A House is Built for Eeyore

EGMONT

EGMONT
We bring stories to life

A House is Built for Eeyore adapted from
The House at Pooh Corner, first published 1928
Published in this edition in 2019 by Egmont UK Limited
The Yellow Building, 1 Nicholas Road, London W11 4AN
www.egmont.co.uk

Text by A.A.Milne copyright © Trustees of the Pooh Properties
Line illustrations copyright © E.H.Shepard
Colouring of the illustrations copyright © 1970 and 1974
E.H.Shepard and Egmont UK Limited

ISBN 978 1 4052 8662 6
67168/001

Printed in Malaysia

A House is Built for Eeyore

A.A.MILNE

with decorations by E.H.Shepard

ORIGINAL AND UNABRIDGED

One day when Pooh Bear had nothing else to do, he thought he would do something, so he went round to Piglet's house to see what Piglet was doing. It was still snowing as he stumped over the white forest track, and he expected to find Piglet warming his toes in front of his fire, but to his surprise he saw that the door was open, and the more he looked inside the more Piglet wasn't there.

'He's out,' said Pooh sadly. 'That's

what it is. He's not in. I shall
have to go on a fast Thinking Walk by
myself. Bother!'

But first he thought that he would
knock very loudly just to make *quite* sure
... and while he waited for Piglet not to
answer, he jumped up and down to keep
warm, and a hum came suddenly
into his head, which seemed
to him a Good Hum, such
as is Hummed Hopefully
to Others.

The more it snows
    (Tiddely pom),
The more it goes
    (Tiddely pom),
The more it goes
    (Tiddely pom),
On snowing.
And nobody knows
    (Tiddely pom),
How cold my toes
    (Tiddely pom),
How cold my toes
    (Tiddely pom),
Are growing.

'So what I'll do,' said Pooh, 'is I'll do this. I'll just go home first and see what the time is, and perhaps I'll put a muffler round my neck, and then I'll go and see Eeyore and sing it to him.'

He hurried back to his own house; and his mind was so busy on the way with the hum that he was getting ready for Eeyore that, when he suddenly saw Piglet sitting in his best arm-chair, he could only stand there rubbing his head and wondering whose house he was in.

'Hallo, Piglet,' he said. 'I thought you were out.'

'No,' said Piglet, 'it's you who were out, Pooh.'

'So it was,' said Pooh. 'I knew one of us was.'

He looked up at his clock, which had stopped at five minutes to eleven some weeks ago.

'Nearly eleven o'clock,' said Pooh happily. 'You're just in time for a little smackerel of something,' and he put his head into the cupboard. 'And then we'll go out, Piglet, and sing my song to Eeyore.'

'Which song, Pooh?'

'The one we're going to sing to Eeyore,' explained Pooh.

The clock was still saying five minutes to eleven when Pooh and Piglet set out on their way half an hour later. The wind had dropped, and the snow, tired of rushing round in circles trying to catch itself up, now fluttered gently down until

it found a place on which to rest, and sometimes the place was Pooh's nose and sometimes it wasn't, and in a little while Piglet was wearing a white muffler round his neck and feeling more snowy behind the ears than he had ever felt before.

'Pooh,' he said at last, and a little timidly, because he didn't want Pooh to think he was Giving In, 'I was just wondering. How would it be if we went home now and *practised* your song, and then sang it to Eeyore tomorrow – or –

or the next day, when we happen to see him?'

'That's a very good idea, Piglet,' said Pooh. 'We'll practise it now as we go along. But it's no good going home to practise it, because it's a special Outdoor Song which Has To Be Sung In The Snow.'

'Are you sure?' asked Piglet anxiously.

'Well, you'll see, Piglet, when you listen. Because this is how it begins.

13

The more it snows, tiddely pom –'

'Tiddely what?' said Piglet.

'Pom,' said Pooh. 'I put that in to make it more hummy. *The more it goes, tiddely pom, the more –*

'Didn't you say snows?'

'Yes, but that was *before.*'

'Before the tiddely pom?'

'It was a *different* tiddely pom,' said Pooh, feeling rather muddled now.

'I'll sing it to you properly and then you'll see.'

14

So he sang it again.

> *The more it*
> *SNOWS~tiddely~pom*
> *The more it*
> *GOES~tiddely~pom*
> *The more it*
> *GOES~tiddely~pom*
> *On*
> *Snowing.*

And nobody
KNOWS~tiddely~pom,
How cold my
TOES~tiddely~pom
How cold my
TOES~tiddely~pom
Are
Growing.

He sang it like that, which is much the best way of singing it, and when he had finished, he waited for Piglet to say

that, of all the Outdoor Hums for Snowy
Weather he had ever heard, this was the
best. And, after thinking the matter out
carefully, Piglet said:

'Pooh,' he said solemnly, 'it isn't the
toes so much as the *ears*.'

By this time they were getting near
Eeyore's Gloomy Place, which was where
he lived, and as it was still very snowy
behind Piglet's ears, and he was
getting tired of it, they turned
into a little pine-wood, and sat

17

down on the gate which led into it. They were out of the snow now, but it was very cold, and to keep themselves warm they sang Pooh's song right through six times, Piglet doing the tiddely-poms and Pooh doing the rest of it, and both of them thumping on the top of the gate with pieces of stick at the proper places. And in a little while they felt much warmer, and were able to talk again.

'I've been thinking,' said Pooh, 'and what I've been thinking about is this. I've

been thinking about Eeyore.'
    'What about Eeyore?'

'Well, poor Eeyore has nowhere to live.'

'Nor he has,' said Piglet.

'*You* have a house, Piglet, and I have a house, and they are very good houses. And Christopher Robin has a house, and Owl and Kanga and Rabbit have houses, and even Rabbit's friends and relations have houses or somethings, but poor Eeyore has nothing. So what I've been thinking is: Let's build him a house.'

'That,' said Piglet, 'is a Grand Idea.

Where shall we build it?'

'We will build it here,' said Pooh, 'just by this wood, out of the wind, because this is where I thought of it. And we will call this Pooh Corner. And we will build an Eeyore House with sticks at Pooh Corner for Eeyore.'

'There was a heap of sticks on the other side of the wood,' said Piglet. 'I saw them. Lots and lots. All piled up.'

'Thank you, Piglet,' said Pooh. 'What you have just said will be a Great Help

to us, and because of it I could call this place Poohanpiglet Corner if Pooh Corner didn't sound better, which it does, being smaller and more like a corner. Come along.'

So they got down off the gate and went round to the other side of the wood to fetch the sticks.

* * *

Christopher Robin had spent the morning indoors going to Africa and back, and he had just got off the boat and was wondering what it was like outside, when who should come knocking at the door but Eeyore.

'Hallo, Eeyore,' said Christopher Robin, as he opened the door and came out. 'How are you?'

'It's snowing still,' said Eeyore gloomily.

'So it is.'

'*And* freezing.'

'Is it?'

'Yes,' said Eeyore. 'However,' he said,

brightening up a little, 'we haven't had an earthquake lately.'

'What's the matter, Eeyore?'

'Nothing, Christopher Robin. Nothing important. I suppose you haven't seen a

house or what-not anywhere about?'

   'What sort of a house?'

   'Just a house.'

   'Who lives there?'

'I do. At least I thought I did. But I suppose I don't. After all, we can't all have houses.'

'But, Eeyore, I didn't know – I always thought –'

'I don't know how it is, Christopher Robin, but what with all this snow and one thing and another, not to mention icicles and such ~like, it isn't so Hot in my field about three o'clock in the morning as some people think it is. It isn't Close, if you know what I mean – not so as

27

to be uncomfortable. It isn't Stuffy. In fact, Christopher Robin,' he went on in a loud whisper, 'quite ~ between ~ ourselves ~ and ~ don't ~ tell ~ any ~ body, it's Cold.'

'Oh, Eeyore!'

'And I said to myself: The others will be sorry if I'm getting myself all cold. They haven't got Brains, any of them, only grey fluff that's blown into their heads by mistake, and they don't Think, but if it goes on snowing for another six

weeks or so, one of them will begin to say to himself: "Eeyore can't be so very much too Hot about three o'clock in the morning." And then it will Get About. And they'll be Sorry.'

'Oh, Eeyore!' said Christopher Robin, feeling very sorry already.

'I don't mean you, Christopher Robin. You're different. So what it all comes to is that I built myself a house down by my little wood.'

'Did you really? How exciting!'

'The really exciting part,' said Eeyore in his most melancholy voice, 'is that when I left it this morning it was there, and when I came back it wasn't. Not at all, very natural, and it was only Eeyore's house. But still I just wondered.'

Christopher Robin didn't stop to

wonder. He was already back in *his* house, putting on his waterproof hat, his waterproof boots, and his waterproof macintosh as fast as he could.

'We'll go and look for it at once,' he called out to Eeyore.

'Sometimes,' said Eeyore, 'when people have quite finished taking a person's house, there are one or two bits which they don't want and are rather glad for the person to take back, if you know what I mean. So I thought if we just went –'

'Come on,' said Christopher Robin, and off they hurried, and in a very little time they got to the corner of the field by the side of the pine-wood, where Eeyore's house wasn't any longer.

'There!' said Eeyore. 'Not a stick of it left! Of course, I've still got all this snow to do what I like with. One mustn't complain.'

But Christopher Robin wasn't listening to Eeyore, he was listening to something else.

'Can you hear it?' he asked.

'What is it? Somebody laughing?'

'Listen.'

They both listened ... and they heard a deep gruff voice saying in a singing voice that the more it snowed the more it went on snowing, and a small high voice tiddely-pomming in between.

'It's Pooh,' said Christopher Robin excitedly ...

'Possibly,' said Eeyore.

'*And* Piglet!' said Christopher Robin excitedly.

'Probably,' said Eeyore. 'What we want is a Trained Bloodhound.'

The words of the song changed suddenly.

'*We've finished our HOUSE!*' sang the gruff voice.

'*Tiddely pom!*' sang the squeaky one.

'*It's a beautiful HOUSE ...* '

'*Tiddely pom ...* '

'*I wish it were MINE ...* '

'Tiddely pom ... '

'Pooh!' shouted Christopher Robin ...

The singers on the gate stopped suddenly.

'It's Christopher Robin!' said Pooh eagerly.

'He's round by the place where we got all those sticks from,' said Piglet.

'Come on,' said Pooh.

They climbed down their gate and hurried round the corner of the wood, Pooh making welcoming noises all the way.

'Why, here *is* Eeyore,' said Pooh, when

36

he had finished hugging Christopher Robin, and he nudged Piglet, and Piglet nudged him, and they thought to themselves what a lovely surprise they had got ready. 'Hallo, Eeyore.'

'Same to you, Pooh Bear, and twice on Thursdays,' said Eeyore gloomily.

Before Pooh could say: 'Why Thursdays?' Christopher Robin began to explain the sad story of Eeyore's Lost House. And Pooh and Piglet listened, and their eyes seemed to get bigger and bigger.

'*Where* did you say it was?' asked Pooh.

'Just here,' said Eeyore.

'Made of sticks?'

'Yes.'

'Oh!' said Piglet.

'What?' said Eeyore.

'I just said "Oh!"' said Piglet nervously. And so as to seem quite at ease he hummed tiddely-pom once or twice in a what-shall-we-do-now kind of way.

'You're sure it *was* a house?' said Pooh.

'I mean, you're sure the house was just here?'

'Of course I am,' said Eeyore. And he murmured to himself, 'No brain at all, some of them.'

'Why, what's the matter, Pooh?' asked Christopher Robin.

'Well,' said Pooh ... 'The fact *is*,' said Pooh ... 'Well, the fact *is*,' said Pooh ... 'You see,' said Pooh ... 'It's like this,' said Pooh, and something seemed to tell him

40

that he wasn't explaining very well, and he nudged Piglet again.

'It's like this,' said Piglet quickly ... 'Only warmer,' he added after deep thought.

'What's warmer?'

'The other side of the wood, where Eeyore's house is.'

'My house?' said Eeyore. 'My house was here.'

'No,' said Piglet firmly. 'The other side of the wood.'

'Because of being warmer,' said Pooh.

'But I ought to *know* –'

'Come and look,' said Piglet simply, and he led the way.

'There wouldn't be *two* houses,' said Pooh. 'Not so close together.'

They came round the corner, and there was Eeyore's house, looking as comfy as anything.

'There you are,' said Piglet.

'Inside as well as outside,' said Pooh proudly.

Eeyore went inside ... and came out again.

'It's a remarkable thing,' he said. 'It *is* my house, and I built it where I said I did, so the wind must have blown it here. And the wind blew it right over the wood, and blew it down here, and here it is as good as ever. In fact, better in places.'

'Much better,' said Pooh and Piglet together.

'It just shows what can be done by

taking a little trouble,' said Eeyore. 'Do you see, Pooh? Do you see, Piglet? Brains first and then Hard Work. Look at it! *That's* the way to build a house,' said Eeyore proudly.

*   *   *

So they left him in it; and Christopher Robin went back to lunch with his friends Pooh and Piglet, and on the way they told him of the Awful Mistake they had made. And when he had finished laughing, they all sang the Outdoor Song for Snowy Weather the rest of the way home, Piglet, who was still not quite sure of his voice, putting in the tiddely~poms again.

'And I know it *seems* easy,' said Piglet to himself, 'but it isn't *every one* who could do it.'

The End

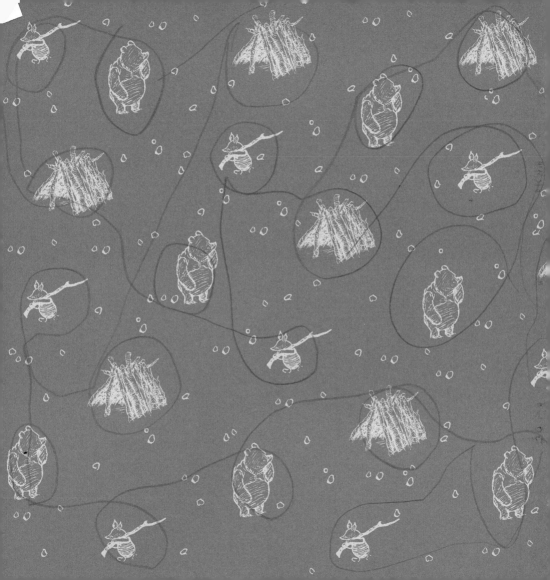